First let me introduce myself. Not my real name of course. I don't want to be exposed as a speaker of the truth and held up as a demigod by the down-trodden workers of betting shops. I merely wish to throw some much-needed light on the dark and mysterious happenings on a high street near you. It may be that you are a customer, in which case this little tome is a complete work of fiction and you are right in thinking that staff are eternally grateful for your custom as you do, in fact, "pay our wages". If you are a customer, please don't read the next couple of sentences as it's not for you and will make you go blind.

Have they gone? Jesus, they get everywhere don't they? Nosey little bastards. Now then my real target audience let's get to know each other. This is a little guide for new starters full of hope and optimism for your career in the betting industry. This book will give you all the training you need so put down that training manual and read on. Or perhaps you're a lifer just like me reminiscing about the "good old days" when we would wield a red settling pen like Sooty wielded his wand. You may just be extremely nosey, sorry I mean curious, about what really goes on behind the scenes in a betting shop or have a close friend or family member who spends hours at their local shop and want to get a glimpse of what they actually get up to. Whatever your motivation for reading this little tome I invite you to sit back, relax and be enlightened, enthralled and just a little bit astounded.

The Secret Life of Betting Shops

Now, I have a confession to make and I need you to take a deep breath before I divulge it. Ok? Ready? Here goes…. I'm middle management.

There. I've said it and I can't take it back. Now let's deal with it and move on. I'm not your typical boss in that I'm actually not a complete twat (even though I've just called myself a boss which is a bit twatty. Sorry). I've got where I am today, which really isn't anywhere to shout about, by hard work, dedication and sheer stubbornness and have worked in betting shops for over twenty years. If you're reading this in work don't forget to put your coin tray in front of your till which is the universal betting shop sign for "Don't mither me"

I have worked for several betting companies and this book is about all of them and none of them. The characters are purely fictitious and none of what you're about to read ever actually happened and is simply the product of my overactive imagination. Trust me. I'm a bookie.

In the first chapter we are going to look at the unique language of the betting shops. Read and learn, folks. Read and learn.

Now I've never known an industry enjoy an acronym more than this one. Consider, if you will, the madness of this conversation;

"Hi. It's John. I'm the GSM and I'll be in charge of signing you off as ASM. Have you been through the ASSIST training? There's a new SEA on the portal but it's a MOSES so you've probably never seen him. Looking at the KPI's it's clear the shop is doing well but we need to be sure there are no POCA concerns. If there are then we have to report it to the MLRO who will complete a SAR. We may have to ask for SOI and make sure they aren't a PEP. Are you comfortable doing the EOD on the CnP, FOBT's and SSBT's? And you can find your way around the BOPC? Great"

Who knew that for minimum wage one had to learn a whole new language? And don't be thinking that you can use any of these new words in Scrabble as it's only the select few that will accept them as a legitimate word. Ah yes, the chosen few. You and I and the other battle-weary soldiers who button up our shirts every day and go toe to toe with the betting public. More about them later. Much more.

ASSIST. That's a long one isn't it? And nobody ever remembers the third S. So, let's break it down.

APPROACH – see that aggressive looking bugger over there having it out with the machine? Yep that's him. The one who keeps glaring at you and pacing back and forth like a demented panther. You need to approach him. Yes, I know his eyes have glazed over and he's slightly frothing at the mouth, but A is for APPROACH.

STAY CALM - well done you've made it out from behind the sanctity of the bandit screen and are now face to face with the panther. Oh, his eyes do look a bit strange, don't they? Oh, and he's doing that whole baring of the teeth thing. No matter. STAY CALM. This is no time to panic. Sure, he's angry and his veins are bulging out but he's not *actually* the Hulk, is he?

SUGGEST – why don't you SUGGEST he takes a little break? A restorative five-minute sit down. You could make him a cup of tea. Maybe offer him a hobnob or two. Always nice to have a little dunk. You don't think he looks like a hobnob would help? Not sure you're qualified to make that decision.

INTERACT – now you've opened up the lines of communication let's keep the INTERACTion going. You feel like a hostage negotiator? That's a bit dramatic. You're just having a little chat to make sure he's ok and isn't spending more than he can afford to lose.

SUPPORT – he needs to know that you're there for him if he ever needs to talk. Yes, even if 2 virtual races, a dog and a bingo are going off. Our social responsibility takes priority over everything. Now has he unfurled his fists yet. There seems to be a red rash creeping up his neck and his face is turning an angry shade of puce. You might want to gauge if you'd beat him in a level start sprint to the counter.

TAKE RESPONSIBILITY – well you're on your own here. It was your decision to leave the counter area. But when, and if, you make it back to your till LOG IT.

POCA

Ah here comes GSM John again

The Secret Life of Betting Shops

"Now then, it's really great that your shop is performing well and you're smashing the hell out of your budget but are we comfortable with where the money is coming from? Let's have a look at the monitored customer list. Stranger, Stranger 2, Stranger 3, 4 and 5, Passing Trade, Hi Viz, Small Asian Man, Tall Asian Man, Ginge, Young Lad, Young Lad Footy, Price Pincher, Tosser, Ugly Bald Guy, Polite Man, Rolf Harris. Rolf Harris?

"He looks like him"

"Okay then. Sexy Steve, Scarface, Uncle Fester, Don Corleone. Don Corleone? Does he look like him?"

"Not at all"

"Then why is he called Don Corleone?"

"He's the head of an organised crime gang round here"

"Oh. Better have a look at his figures then. Right in the last quarter he's staked £600,000 with returns of £350,000. So, he's losing £250,000 to us"

"And he's a machine player too. And so are his crew"

"His crew?" John asks

"Yeah his hangers on. You know his drivers and "droppers"

"Right. Right. So, we should probably ask for SOI"

"What?"

"Source of Income" John explains

The Secret Life of Betting Shops

"Oh yeah. Good luck with that"

"When I say we…."

"I'm not asking him. I've lived all my life with ten fingers and two functioning kneecaps, and I'd like to keep it that way"

Door Chime Sounds

"There he is now. Why don't *you* have a little interaction with him?" the manager says

"Well let's not be too hasty" John ducks behind the till "I mean, of course it's important to be compliant but we don't want to jump to conclusions, do we? We don't know for certain he's a wrong 'un do we? Nasty looking scar he has on his face isn't it? And what does his tattoo say? The one on his neck?"

"Dealer" the shop manager replies

"Really?" John raises an eyebrow "Who would have that on their neck? A croupier maybe?"

"Oh yeah" the manager says "It's a new trend to have your occupation tattooed on. I'm booked in to have ASS MAN inked on to my arm next week. My wife's not happy about it but what can you do?"

"Right. Well let's just monitor the situation for now okay?"

"Okay. You're the boss"

KPI's

The Secret Life of Betting Shops

Right the KPI's. Key Performance Indicators. Basically, how your shop is performing in key areas of the business namely stakes, FOBT turnover and profit. Look after these little badgers and John et al will be fawning over you like a modern-day deity. Nothing makes John happier than basking, lizard like, in someone else's glory. It's all about reflected brilliance. You make him look good, he makes his boss look good and everyone's happy. Of course, if your KPI's are good you won't really hear about it but if they're bad then expect a prolonged period of pressure giving rise to Hurricane Shitstorm. Sorry went a bit weather reader then.

FOBT's

Ah the devil's own playthings.

"Their heart is faithless. Now they must bear their guilt. The LORD will break down their altars and destroy their sacred pillars. **Hosea 10:2**

I'm pretty sure that the pillars referred to are, in fact, FOBT's. Fixed Odds Betting Terminals. A modern-day plague sent to wreak havoc and bring misery to the masses. All those that play them shall be tainted.

"For the love of money is a root of all sorts of evil, and some by longing for it have wandered away from the faith and pierced themselves with many griefs" Timothy 6:10

Pretty scary stuff huh? Are you wondering if this also includes demo play? Hang on I'll go back to the scriptures....

"Though they know God's decree that those who practice such things deserve to die, they not only do them but give approval to those who practice them. Revelation 21:4

Hang on the phone's ringing,

"Hi. It's John. I'm going to ask you some questions about this week's new game launch. Can you tell me what it's called?

"Err is it We're All Going to Hell in A Handcart?" the manager asks

"What"?

"No wait a minute. It's we're all going to hell in a handcart with free spins"

"What the hell….?" John says

"Please don't mention hell. I'm very vulnerable right now. I've persuaded old Jack to have a go of Magic Mermaids and probably cast him asunder for all eternity. He only wanted a Trixie"

I better move on to a different acronym before this crisis of conscience becomes crippling. We will return to these vicious little cash cows later.

SSBT's

Ah that's better. SSBT's. A machine that doesn't have the devil on speed dial. An innocuous little add on sat quietly in the shop minding its own business. Or is it? Isn't it possible that this newcomer could be sent to replace us?

The Secret Life of Betting Shops

Imagine a cashier that doesn't have cash differences, doesn't get conned, never goes sick, never late, doesn't overpay bets and doesn't need 20-minute break every 6 hours. Well that's what this is. SSBT is for Self Service Betting Terminal. It's the quiet ones you have to watch. You have been warned.

BP/BOG/EP/SP/EMP

Oh, just be happy if your 12 scrawly Yankees win at all and stop being a bloody nuisance with your best price this and your guaranteed best odds race that. And, yes, I do know scrawly isn't a word but picture, if you will, a spider who has dipped all his legs in an ink pot then scurried across a betting slip. Imagine, then, said spider approaching the weary cashier and asking for a price on said scrawl. Feck off Incey you can have SP.

Now we know a little betting parlay why don't we take a look at the actual product we sell?

Do you know your Dundee Shuffle from your Round the Clock? Can you explain why a non-runner on a round robin gives nil returns? Can you perm any 4 from 7? No? Well you'll fit right in with the vast majority of betting shop staff who also wouldn't know their arse from their elbow. Or their trixie from their patent.

I'll tell you who does have impeccable, to the penny, betting knowledge though. Customers. Oh yes, their knowledge and ability to settle their own bets is second to none. Many betting slips are handed in with the returns already calculated thus negating the need for sophisticated settling software at all. Sophisticated Settling Software. I've just invented a new acronym. That's just what we needed. Next time a customer gives you the "That's not right" line tell him that the SSS says it is so and, therefore, it is so. Do make sure you haven't translated the bet wrong though as that way lies embarrassment and a helping of humble pie and we all know that shop staff don't get time to eat.

For those amongst you not yet indoctrinated in the ways of the betting shop I should explain what is meant by the term "translated".

Basically, a member of the betting public can, and usually does, write any old shite on a betting slip and the SSS will not be able to read it. For all the till knows it could be a horse in the 3.30 at Kempton, Shakespeare's fifth sonnet or be completely blank and, believe me, some staff would still accept it. The till will settle all the bets according to the results that are sent to it but, if the staff, translate a bet wrong the return will be wrong. What happens is that staff have to "tell" the till what is on each bet and what type of bet the customer wants. Sounds straightforward enough doesn't it? For most staff it is and mistakes are few but there are some right dozy gits that are forever entering an incorrect selection, wrong price or translating as a win instead of an ew and making life infinitely harder for their colleagues who have to rectify their mistakes whilst being stared at by the wronged customer who has planted his feet at the counter and is refusing to move until said dispute is resolved.

In the all too common event of a bet dispute many customers, usually the older ones, will produce a dog-eared, well-thumbed ready reckoner (look it up) from their arse pocket and, with self-indulgent smugness about how clever they are, proceed to explain how the bet is settled. They will also intersperse said maths lesson with their opinions on the SSS and how they have "been having the same bet for 37 years and it's always settled wrong in this shop". The more observant shop staff will disappear into the kitchen area when they see them approaching. In some situations, there is no comradeship amongst colleagues. This same selfishness is also displayed when Margaret comes in with her 342 lottery slips. Staff can be halfway through a conversation and one of them will suddenly disappear mid-sentence. As the old adage goes work smart not hard. Oh, and always bag the till with the best view of the door so you can scarper if you see the possibility of having to do a bit of work coming into the shop.

When I first started in this industry, in the mid 1990's, one had to jump, blindfold, through burning hoops with both legs tied together before anyone would let you anywhere near the shop keys. Nowadays we have an abundance of "latchkey kids" who wouldn't have got a look in twenty years ago. This new breed of "manager" are almost clone-like in their similarities. Surly expressions, mostly dead behind the eyes and between the ears with all the aplomb and charm of a used tissue. Bit harsh I hear you say. As exhibit A I would like to present the following telephone conversation;

"Hi. It's Cath. I've got a problem with a bet"

"Yes?" I respond.

"It's late" says Cath

"How late?" I ask

Cath doesn't know how late. Cath is in her shop surrounded by all sorts of technology that could tell her exactly how late the bet is.

"Well can you have a look please as I'm driving?"

A full minute ticks by.

"It's 12 seconds late" Cath says

"And how long was the race?"

Cath doesn't know how long. Cath is in her shop surrounded by technology that could tell her exactly how long the race was.

"Well I'll need to know before I make a decision"

Another minute ticks by. It's amazing what the brain can conjure up in 60 seconds. I am wondering how Cath functions in her daily life.

"One metre" she says

"What?" I laugh despite myself

"One metre" she says again

"A metre?"

"Yes" she says "One M"

Mother. Of. God.

"That's a mile" I say

"Oh" says Cath

"What is it?" I jest "longest leg wins?"

Cath is one of many "managers" whose stupidity and industry ignorance is completely off the scales. Some of you will think that this is down to training and that the Company doesn't invest in its staff and expects too much. To that I say 'Bollocks'. There are some people in this world whose cheese slid off their crackers way before they started work. These cranially challenged half-wits make everybody else's job harder just by turning up.

If you still have your heart set on a career in the betting industry, ask yourself if this is really the job for you.

I am frequently amazed by how many betting shop staff have absolutely no interest in sport and do wonder how much more they might enjoy the job if they had half a clue what was going on around them. There are not many jobs where you get to watch sport all day every day and, if the studio is having an off day, you can't in this job either but can often watch Judge Judy and Jeremy Kyle.

As I write this in my office at the back of a shop (on my lunch break. Ahem) I can hear the beginnings of a dispute between the shop manager and a disgruntled customer whose bet is late. The shop manager is, apparently, "out of order" and so much so that the customer tells him at least half a dozen times. He then proceeds to tell the rest of the shop's customers just how out of order he is. What this odious, jumped up dipshit doesn't tell them is that he had over four hours to place his bet but, in true punter style, waits until the stalls open before putting his bet on. Now I know what you're thinking and you're right. The shop manager *should* have made a phone call to Catterick and insisted that all 12 horses be put back in the stalls so that said dipshit would not have his day, maybe even his entire life by the way he's carrying on, ruined by the injustice of being told his bet is late.

Why must customers do that? What is this compulsion to leave it to the absolute last second, and beyond, to place their bets? Do they carry this habit into every aspect of their lives? When eating a roast dinner do they leave the food on the plate until the very last second before it goes cold then shovel it all in? Do they wait until the supermarket is 5 minutes from closing then race round doing the "big shop" in a punter's version of Supermarket

Sweep? Do they hold their pee in for hours until their teeth hurt, and they are just about to piss themselves before going for a slash? Actually, judging by the state of betting shop toilet floors I think they actually do that last one but get their timings all wrong (and their aim)

Customer Tip #1 – Don't be a last-minute Larry

As refusal can often offend

Don't be a last-minute Larry

It drives staff round the bend

I only wish betting shops existed in Shakespearian times. What rich material old Will could have gleaned from the carnival that is the betting shop. Back when I was a frontline shop soldier (try saying that 3 times) it was like Sunday Night at the Palladium with act after act exhibiting their unique "quirks".

Roll up roll up to see the "Invisible Horse" show. Watch in amazement as Harry rides a pretend horse over the sticks. The equine version of air guitar. Gasp as Richard walks sideways like a crab as he makes his horse go faster leaning like the Tower of Pisa. See how he walks into Harry as he does and they both end up on their arses.

Marvel at the mis-direction of Barry Conway and his backing group The Conmen as they practice their dark magic in front of your very eyes.

Applaud, if you will, the skilled pen throwers who decorate the ceiling tiles with little blue stalactites (or should that be stalagmites?)

And an ovation, please, for the greatest act of them all. The smiles on the face of the staff.

Mis-direction indeed.

I remember managing a Moss Side betting shop in the late 90's and blessing myself with the holy cross before I went in. For those not graced by Mancunian heritage, or those with a piss poor knowledge of UK geography, Moss Side is a suburb of Manchester. Suburb may conjure up images of neatly mown grass and white picket fences. The only fences in Moss Side were those handling stolen goods and they weren't just white. The only grass anyone took any interest in was the smoking variety. You get the picture. It was a multi-cultural war zone. I loved it.

Picture this. A Moss Side betting shop circa 1999. Full of smoke, some of it, shall we say, on the "fragrant" side. Jamaican "yardies" (their term not mine) occupying one set of state of the art "cinema style seating" (a fancy term for shitty seats with worn pads, unspeakable stains and a writing shelf at the back used to roll joints) and the Asian Massif (nobody's term but sums these wannabes up nicely) on the other. I watch from my elevated position behind the screen like a guard overlooking a prison yard waiting for the inevitable kick-off. My inmates don't disappoint. They bounce around the shop as if they have 4 inches of mattress strapped to their shoes reading the form like they know what the fuck all those numbers mean. Ah here we go, I think, the first dog race of the day. This will be fun.

As they do every day six of them, from opposite sides of da 'hood, crowd round one sheet of paper pinned to the wall at great expense of my thumb-pad. The jostling begins. The looking up and down has started. There is much baring of teeth and tutting sounds. They remind me of those people that only communicate in clicks. I watch as the dogs are loaded into the traps. The bell sounds to let normal people know the hare is running and to get your bet on. Now. These are not normal fucking people. Oh no. These bastards wait until the very last second then race, en masse, to the counter faster than the hare itself. Fortunately I have the fastest cashiers in the West and all but one of the bets gets on. The winning one. For fucks sake. I emerge from behind the settling desk and lock stares with the punter who is now holding me personally responsible for the fact that he is a dickhead. I tell him what I tell all of them every single day. At least twice. Get your bet on earlier. He doesn't want to hear my words. Apparently I am a "Bombaclot". As is the way with most staff/customer "debates" the whole of the shop seems to have an opinion on this. And guess what? The kangaroo court has found in favour of.........the soft twat customer too fucking slow to get to the counter in time. Street and gang rivalries are temporarily put on ice as they unite in their assertion that I am, in fact, a bombaclot. My cashiers and I, all female, hold our ground. Leonidas had nothing on us. We reach the usual impasse, the Mexican standoff, the unwillingness of either party to back down. This bullshit goes on for ten minutes until he walks away from the counter, backwards, pointing and telling me he'll see me outside later. Oh please walk into a fucking chair you annoying, sniveling, needy little twat.

I return back behind my desk, pick up my trusty red settling pen and bed in for the next 10 fun-filled hours.

God I loved that bloody shop.

And now, over 20 years later, I'm still in the game (not to be confused with on the game) and punters still can't get their bets on in time.

Blimey. 24 years I've been in this wondrous, crazy, mind boggling madness of a career. I remember when it all began….

1995. February. Me, a fresh (spotty) faced 18 year old, wanting to earn a few pennies before embarking on university life. I'm off to Warwick University and I'm going to be a lawyer, a solicitor, a journalist, an author. I'm clever. I'm really clever. I'm so clever I could have gone to Oxford but they didn't do the course I wanted. Until I go to university I will work in a betting shop, Stanley Racing, as a "Saturday Girl". I might even do a couple of nights if the mood takes me. I breeze through the interview. I push open the door to the shop on my first Saturday. Fuck. What have I done? This shop is nothing like the one I was interviewed in. When I pass the bar (the legal one not the drinks one) I'll sue these bastards for misrepresentation. I wait by the counter door whilst the manager unlocks several bolts to let me in. Jesus. This shop is in Old Trafford not far from United's ground and next door to a tram station. Today United are at home. Oh fuck. I enquire of my manager as to who is training me and he replies it is him. Great. He is a miserable, surly fucker (I later marry him. He didn't change).

At 1pm all hell breaks loose. The match crowd come in. They are asking me things I don't understand. I'm off to get a degree in French so I'm good at languages but I've never heard of the one they're speaking. I later become an expert at drunken betting parlay. At 3pm the shop has quietened so I sit down. I start spinning on my chair. The surly one has his head down reading the Daily Mail. I start to fidget. There is gum under the counter. Gross. There is also a red button. I press it. It's not my fault. Not really. I didn't know it was a panic button. Not until two police officers burst in a few minutes later. For fucks sake. The surly one is not amused. He tells me to count the cash in my till. I do. I transfer it to him. He counts it. There are three fake £20 notes. He is even less amused now. Jesus. What a first day.

You know how I said I'm really clever? Scratch that. All these years later I'm still here speaking the betting language whilst the wonderful, romantic French language slips from memory. Merde.

If I could tell my 18 year old self to stay away from betting shops would I? Could I? Not on your life. It would have been useful, however, to have a little no holes barred guide to betting shops such as this one so that I didn't end up crying like a fanny the first time a customer was mean to me.

 Speaking of customers there will be some who stay with you long after you, or they, have moved on. One of my all-time favourite customers was Joe.

Picture this. Salford betting shop. 1996. Long before the smoking ban. I sometimes wonder how many non-smoking staff contracted lung cancer from being in close quarters with smoking colleagues for so many hours a day. I'm glad to say I didn't get lung cancer. No, I got breast cancer. But that's a story for a different day.

I had survived, barely, my baptism of betting shop fire, in Old Trafford and Moss Side and was, ahem, rewarded with this gig in Salford. The shop was huge with dual entrances so that the punters could stage a pincer like attack. One customer, Old Joe, used to enjoy coming through one door, walking twice round the central pillar and out through the other door. 3 times he would perform this ritual and more if there was a gap in racing (oooh who remembers gaps in racing?)

Joe was the local eccentric off the Duchy estate and he was fabulous. Most days he would come in wearing an ill-fitted brown suit with a V-neck jumper underneath, the trousers not quite reaching his ankles and tied round the waist with a piece of string. He patently took his hair inspiration from Don King and he had dispensed with wearing his false teeth years before. He had the craziest stare of anyone I've ever met and fingernails the colour of a brown paper bag. In all honesty he should probably have been in some sort of institution and looked after by the state but they hadn't quite caught up with him by that stage. When he started sunbathing naked in his garden whilst having a bit of a fidget they eventually took him away. But, for now, we had him most days. He came in through the far door. Walked across the shop towards the pillar, looked straight at the counter "What are you looking at you bastards?"

"Ah. Morning Joe" we replied.

Joe would bet whatever he had in his tatty pocket. I'd seen him bet £50 and I'd taken a bet from him for 24p. If he won big he would tip. If he was on his arse he'd ask for the tip back. You have to remember all this was in the days before the Gambling Commission compiled its modern day version of the Ten Commandments. "Joe, thou shalt stop when the fun stops" would have been met with "Shut up you bastard"

Another trait of betting shop customers is that annoying habit they have of giving you all their previous day/week/month/year's betting slips, in various states of tattiness, with the ubiquitous line "Can you check if there's anything on them?"

Customer Tip #2 – You know full well they're losers

And are hoping we've made a mistake

So put them in the bloody bin

And give us all a break

Other overused punter phrases include, but are not limited to, the following;

1) Are you eating again? – Yes I find I need to do it most days
2) Just a few coppers off that – Don't be offended if you are instantly given 3p
3) You shouldn't be open this late at night – You're right. Please leave
4) Get the wheelbarrow out for this one – The 80's called. They want their joke back

5) You get some holidays you – And unlike you I also have some days in work
6) I looked at that horse – You looked at all of them. Fool
7) Can I get a tea? – Probably. Oh you mean in here?
8) Can I owe you the 5p? – Can I owe you the tea?
9) Any reading glasses I can borrow? – Do we look like Specsavers? Oh you can't see can you?
10) This one's a banker. My mate works in the trainers yard – You have no friends but I'll take your £2 on it anyway

How to be a good customer in ten easy steps;

1) Always have your money ready with the bet – but not on top of it
2) Don't try to get in before opening time
3) If you do try to get in before opening time don't peer through the glass forlornly. It's pathetic.
4) Don't steal the Racing Post or any supplements therein
5) Be clean
6) Be polite
7) Bring in treats every now and then
8) Don't bring us weird stuff or anything homemade

9) Don't ask us work related questions if you see us outside

10) Write your bets clearly as if your very life depended on it

If you are still reading then perhaps you think you have what it takes to work in a betting shop. Perhaps you already do work in a betting shop and are wondering how, even though this is clearly a work of fiction and therefore no legal or disciplinary action must be taken, it manages to be so damn accurate.

Ah disciplinary action. The standard last line of a memo – *failure to follow the above may result in disciplinary action being taken.*

The "above" can be a whole multitude of sins including;

1) Opening a shop late (but not early curiously)
2) Overpaying a bet (but not underpaying curiously)
3) Cash shortages (but not over curiously)
4) Under Banking (but not over banking curiously)
5) Spending too much on demo mode
6) Spending too little on demo mode
7) Doing crap on a promotion

8) Doing well on a promotion by cheating so as to avoid point 7
9) Using your mobile at the counter (checking results is not a valid reason)
10) Telling customers or colleagues to f**k off (even if they totally deserved it)

The possible reasons to be invited to a disciplinary are endless. My personal favourite was the deputy manager who downloaded an app to his phone which switched TVs on and off. Said deputy manager decided to try this app out in the competitors whose screen system he duly shut down. And he would have gotten away with it if it weren't for the pesky CCTV and the fact he was wearing his uniform. Genius.

Of course it's not all staff that are a bit lacking in brain matter and do actually want to give their customers the best possible experience.

I'll tuck my soap box under the desk in a minute but first I'll say this. There is a will in the vast majority of betting industry staff to provide a fun, safe environment for the recreational punter with no desire to turn a blind eye to either problem gambling or to entertain revenue from non-legit sources. A whole world of work goes on behind the scenes to ensure the shops are compliant. And it's not just because the Gambling Commission says we have to. Moreover it is because betting shop staff are decent, honest, moral people. Let's throw some light on that.

You may be surprised to learn that bookies actually stop people gambling with them because they are losing too much. That's right. Losing too much. There are so many processes and resources you can use to ensure the customers in your shop can afford to be there and you will be trained in spotting the signs of problem gambling. I wonder what will happen when these people with issues are forced online away from the trained eyes of shop staff. You may have heard the negative press surrounding FOBT's so let's spend a little time on them whilst we still have them.

As I'm such a dinosaur I remember very well when betting shops had a single fruit machine in them. I remember a prick called Noel who used to come in on his way home from work every night and fill it with 5p's and other assorted "shrapnel" as he called it. "Don't mind a bit of shrapnel do you?" he'd say as he emptied his pockets of as much shite as he could find.

At the end of the night, which in some cases was about 5pm, we had to empty the "hopper" by pressing the hopper dump button. I love that. Hopper dump. It was filled every morning with £125 and, if you were really unlucky, you'd miss the opening of the tube and would spend the next half hour searching for coins. Despite the shortcomings of these one armed bandits they felt honest particularly when compared to their modern day relatives who don't have any arms at all but are far from armless. Sorry.

Fixed Odds Betting Terminals are certainly a controversial bit of kit. There are all sorts of campaign groups lobbying to restrict their stake levels and ease of access. Newspapers seize on inflated turnover figures with little understanding of what they are actually reporting on. Punters with sad faces and hard luck stories pop up on various media with their tales of woe about how these machines have destroyed their lives. One absolute bell-end actually avoided a prison sentence for criminal damage and intimidation basically stating the "machines made me do it" and nobody tried to help him. Whilst I have sympathy for addicts of any vice I can't be doing with some of these tossers playing the victim and blaming staff within the industry for their behaviour. Of course there are gambling addicts. There always has been and there always will be. The difference nowadays is that staff are trained in such matters and, despite what the nay-sayers spout, actually have an appetite to protect players from harm. Can't say that about online gambling can we?

Ode to a FOBT;

> You may have no arms
>
> But you're a bandit nonetheless

I thank you

Update -this section on FOBT's was written before the longest awaited outcome in history of the Triennial Review. We, the workers, are now facing down the barrel of a gun, teetering with uncertainty at the edge of an abyss waiting to see how the dice will fall. The unthinkable has happened. The people have spoken, by people I mean those in Government desperate for a headline, those people who hold betting shops in the same regard as brothels and believe they are righting a wrong by reducing the maximum stake per spin to £2. I do wonder how many of them actually set foot in a licensed betting office and took cognizance of the fine work being done by betting shop staff up and down the land to protect players. I hope they don't regret forcing players online where protection is weak at best. The online operators must still be on a high, watering at the mouth at the thought of all those customers opening new accounts, luring them in with sign up bonuses and VIP status. They will be ready 24/7 to max out credit cards as their expanded flock realize they can actually spin hundreds at a time. The gambling addicts will be all over this. I can bet on a credit card? Really? Multiple credit cards? Any time of the day or night? And nobody will ask if I'm ok or offer me a break? I don't have to interact with anybody? Ever? I can get as drunk as a skunk and spin and spin and spin until? Until what? Well, actually, until you want to withdraw any "winnings" and then you will have to provide I.D, proof of address and send various photographs of depositing cards. Don't worry, though, if that all seems like too much hassle you can just reverse your withdrawal request and carry on spinning!

I realize I'm getting a little preachy but, really, talk about sweeping a problem under the carpet. How sad that the various factions with a vested interest in gambling from operators, mental health workers and treatment providers to the NHS, Gambling Commission and the Treasury couldn't have agreed on a programme of changes that could have had a positive outcome for all concerned and particularly those at risk of harm from problem gambling. The answer to tackling addiction lies in a holistic approach whereby all parties work together in introducing measurable, practical steps to ensure that those who need help are given every opportunity to access it. How do we reach gamblers at 3 o'clock in the morning, half cut and bleary eyed propped up in bed on their smartphone trying to win back that month's mortgage money? If anyone in government is interested in meeting to discuss this then I'm your (wo)man.

Now let's put this aside and get back to the life of betting shop staff whilst we still have betting shops. Pah!

If you have any expectations with this job then this section is aimed at you.

Try not to have any. It's easier that way. Think of your working day as an extended football match in which your team are playing Barcelona in the Champions League Semi Final and you're down to 10 men. Even though you want to get through unscathed chances are you won't. At the end of your shift you will likely trudge, beaten and battle weary, into the cold, dark night air comforted by the knowledge that it's all over. For the next ten hours at least. Low expectations should also be applied when thinking about pay, working conditions and career prospects. Still we don't do this job for the money do we?

Don't worry though as this job still has a little perk that we like to refer to as tips.

Tips. Freebies. Backhanders. Call 'em what you want they are all (mostly) gratefully received. Be prepared to be brought biscuits, sweets and other confectionary from the local discount shop. Always check the best before date before consuming as we all know that customers, like foxes, have no honour. Also make sure that your shop team has a clear and robust tips policy in place as God help you if Janice doesn't get her £3.33 tip when she's back from her day off.

As middle management one of my major bug bears is the amount of sickly staff we seem to have on the books.

 A basic rule of not being a twat of a colleague. If you can come into work then do. Hangovers, toothache, period pain, vomiting, coughing, sneezing, headaches and other such ailments are no reason to leave your workmates in the lurch. I had someone ring up with general malaise once. The fuck is general malaise? Also if you are ringing in sick with a stomach bug there is really no need to do "the voice". The voice only need be deployed when ringing in with a throat related malady. At any other time it is pathetic and makes you sound like a fanny. As does getting your mum/dad/auntie/teacher to call in on your behalf. Man up and get to work.

Now don't get me wrong a betting shop based lifestyle isn't the healthiest in the world so let's look at the physical pitfalls of working in a betting shop. Jaundice is a real risk as, in the winter months, you will likely be arriving and leaving in the hours of darkness. This is not so much of a risk in the height of summer when you can expect to receive, on average, 23 minutes of sunlight per day. I suggest keeping a yellow paint chart by the till so that you can check your jaundice levels on a regular basis.

Should you manage to avoid jaundice it is unlikely you will remain slim (for those of you that started that way). Pandas have bamboo, flamingos have crayfish and betting shop staff have takeaways on every shift.

Some of you may be worried about your physical safety within the shop environment.

Unless you work in a betting shop in a quaint little village in middle England, and I'm not sure they actually exist, then chances are you will be threatened with violence by a member of the betting public. Now your options to deal with said threats are manifold. If you've watched Kill Bill (or maybe Kung Fu Panda would be more appropriate) then you could try employing some kick-ass moves and associated "hiiii-ya" type noises to scare off the would be attacker. If you don't condone violence, or perhaps suffer from arthritic hips, then you can always rely on karma. The risk, as I see it, is that John Lennon's type of karma may have been instant but, for the rest of us, it usually takes a bit longer and you really need it sorting before he "comes back when you close to rip your head off".

Having been involved in betting shops in Manchester and Liverpool for over twenty years I am amazed on an almost daily basis that there aren't more actual, physical scuffles between staff and customers. If there is a more patient, laid back bunch of people than betting shop staff then I've yet to meet them. Shop staff are Teflon coated patron saints of knob heads.

Some of the particularly knobby sort have a penchant for losing their receipt.

Ah here's GSM John again. Was just wondering where he had gotten to. Let's eavesdrop on his telephone conversation with a shop manager.

"John? I've got a customer here who's lost his copy"

"When is it from?" John asks

"The 4.25 at Worcester"

"It's only half four now. How has he lost it? Did he leave the shop?"

"Err...Nope"

"He's stood in earshot no isn't he?" John says

"That's right" replies the manager

"Jesus" mutters John "How much is off it?"

"£650" the manager replies

"Six hundred and fifty quid?" John says slowly

"That's right" the manager says "and he wants paying out now"

"Well that's not going to happen unless he finds his ticket. We need 2 forms of I.D and I'll have to come and sign off on it but it won't be today"

"Well" the manager says "if he doesn't get his money today he's going to trash the shop"

"For fucks sake" exclaims John "he loses his sodding ticket in under 5 minutes and it's somehow our fault"

"Yep" the manager says "Would you like to speak to him?"

"No" says John "I would not like to speak to him"

"Well he wants to speak to you" says the manager "I'll just pass the phone through..."

"No!!" says John "I do not want to speak to the dick. Just tell him that..."

"Who are you calling a dick?" says the dick "Come here and say that. I'll smash *your* face in as well. You know it's my bet. Pay me my fucking money"

GSM John is making a mental note to book himself in for Taekwondo classes.

That's the thing that people don't realise about this job. Certain occupations have an in built, expected level of aggression or threat. Army folk, bouncers, prison officers and traffic wardens all enter into such professions fully aware of the dangers. The unsuspecting sods who get referred to betting shop jobs from employment agencies probably think it's a cushy little retail number sat on their arse all day drinking tea. I often have to remind them that they have to get to management level before that happens.

The Secret Life of Betting Shops

At this juncture I would like to introduce you to your friend and mine. The so called quick slip.

Except they're not. Quick that is. These slips were designed to make life easier but, in reality, may well be the reason you smash your face off the bandit screen repeatedly until blood starts dripping into the scanner. Which will likely exacerbate the problem but may provide you temporary relief. The reason for the frustration may be technical and you will require assistance from the "Helpdesk". The conversation will go like this (after 24 minutes on hold);

"Helpdesk"

"Hi. It's shop 666. My till/scanner/router/printer/screen isn't working"

"Ok. Can you turn it off for twenty minutes then switch it back on?"

"OK. Then what?"

"If that doesn't fix it then call us back"

"OK. I'll speak to you in twenty minutes"

Ode to the Helpdesk;

The Secret Life of Betting Shops

We've tried the off and on,

And it's still on the blink,

So please send an engineer,

As we're really on the brink

If the reason for the mark sense failure isn't due to technical reasons then it will be due to punter reasons. Boxes that should be marked won't be and boxes that shouldn't be marked will be. If they realise their mistake before getting to the counter they will, helpfully, put a line through the error. Yep they'll just cross it out. Which is fine because, obviously, the till is so sophisticated it can tell a correction mark from an intentional mark. Sometimes the customer will use a discarded mark sense slip from the side which may already have pen marks on it. Which is fine because, obviously, the till is so sophisticated it can distinguish one customer's line from another. I really don't know why we need staff at all. In fact stop reading this, get your coat and go home. The customers have got this sorted.

Quick slips are most commonly used for football and numbers betting. Twenty years ago the only lottery people bet on in the shops was the Irish Lottery. I remember, as a shop manager, rolling them all up into a fat tube to settle at home on a Saturday night. It was rather satisfying slashing a big red line through them and the task was rattled off in under thirty minutes. Nowadays the punters are spoilt for choice with betting available on the lotteries of a whole host of countries including Spain, America, Germany, Canada and Azerbaijan. Even the Irish Lottery isn't straight forward anymore. There are draws within draws, 6 number and 7 number draws. It's like a set of Russian dolls only the possibilities never end. If the customers don't want to wait then they can slake their numbers betting thirst with a few go's on the bingo. There is a shop in a salubrious part of Liverpool that takes circa 300 bingo bets a day for a grand total of £30. In the real world you would not associate the punters who place said bets with bingo. You may, or you may not, associate them with petty crime and gang warfare. I couldn't possibly comment but I swear I saw a picture of one of them in the local paper's "Most Wanted" gallery. But between the hours of 8.30am and 10pm they are avid bingo players carefully and diligently marking the numbers off as they are drawn. Al Capone must be turning in his grave.

If you can tolerate the verbal abuse, the acronyms, the betting parlay and the numerous ways a customer can ruin your day then I salute you but have you considered what may be your biggest hurdle yet? The unique, unidentifiable odour of a betting shop.

A staple cupboard essential in any self-respecting betting shop is a can or five of air freshener. Shop staff get through the stuff at an alarming rate and sales must soar during the summer months when pong levels reach a high. Most shops, at one time or another, will have encountered a fragrant customer with the ability to empty a shop in 30 seconds flat. Staff bicker about who is best placed to tackle said whiffy person and I've lost count of the number of times I've been asked how they should handle the situation. Some staff take the direct approach of "you stink" whilst others are a tad more sensitive and will surreptitiously follow behind them perfuming the air with

"Summer Meadow" spray until nobody can actually breathe. The problem is even more delicate when the odour emanates from a fellow staff member. I get even more calls from staff about their colleagues personal hygiene than I do about the customers'.

Rats and mice are another common source of stink and it seems one of their most favourite places to die is in a betting shop. Before they pop their clogs, however, they like to play a little game of hide and seek. The rodents leave little clues, rat shit mostly, to give staff little hints about where they are hiding. When the staff think they have narrowed it down to the little hole in the storeroom – WHAM – up one pops from behind the printer laughing its little legs off as the staff run shrieking from the shop.

If you have an iron constitution and thick skin then you are halfway qualified to succeeding in a betting shop. However, have you factored in the betting shop display guide?

The betting shop display is an abstract work of art clearly designed by a devotee of the Rubik's cube. There seems to be no rhyme or reason to the layout other than to ensure the person putting them up in the morning is left frustrated, puzzled and perplexed. To succeed in the challenge you will need scissors, patience and a logical mind. Comments should be sent to whatthefuckisthismadness@rp.co.uk

FREE BINGO GAME

Five and Five Ones	This is my last bet	It's more than that	One let me down	I'll take a cheque
Do us a tea/coffee	You still here?	Bloody fixed these machines are	It's lovely outside	You pressing that lose button again?
I'll be in with the wheelbarr ow	Can you check that's on?	Have the 49s gone yet?	It's not my bet (usually on a big win)	Have you got a bed in the back?

Now I'm not sure how you came to be employed by a betting shop but it is true to say that, despite national levels of unemployment, the industry always has vacancies.

It all sounds so easy. We need people. People need a job. Said people fill in an application form, perhaps the most serious will even include a covering letter, we interview them, and we appoint them. God's in his heaven, the birds are singing and everybody's happy. Except they never are. Happy that is. Existing staff moan that they have to train them up. New starters moan that they aren't getting the training they were promised and "didn't realise" they would have to work nights and weekends. Don't even start with that shit.

My most favourite application of all time came from a guy who worked in my local pizza shop. This is his largely unedited email to my good self (with identifying details removed. I've been on the GDPR course don't worry about

that)

Thanks for getting in touch.

We get 1 shot at life, After waiting for the right one, I believe my

chance has just landed. (Please read on)

I would be honoured to come and join your team and I guarantee

success. I see myself as one of the most valuable hardworking

people you will ever meet. We can enjoy long success together.

I am 25 years old, currently work 50 hours a week plus, have a

fiance and drive a vauxhall astra.

Even though you only have cashier vacancies I hope we can come to

an agreement and start something potentially special.

I am in line for a big breakthrough in becoming an area manager,

like yourself you had probably worked all your life for that position.

For that chance.

To drop my current role to a cashier from a shop manager earning

24,000 a year to just £6.50 an hour would in most people's eyes seem like a wrong move, but 9 years in the food industry it feels

right to move on and explore new boundaries.

I admire Horse Racing. I admire the customers, I admire the betting

industry.

I am very knowledgeable in your part of the world and I would

probably be one of the best shop managers on your team. I am

hungry for success, I get a buzz out of communicating with the

*public and you can rely on me to deliver (*he did deliver some

scrummy pizza to be fair*)*

I can handle cash, manage a team, settle a lucky 15 manually and

give a presentation on the gambling commission. I tick all the right

boxes.

But the question is could I drop from 24k a year to £6.50 per hour?

Financially I can't no way, could I be in a store as a cashier when I

know I do a better job than the shop manager? It would be hard.

If you could shortlist me for any manager vacancies that would be

The Secret Life of Betting Shops

great.

I hope to speak to you soon. If you want to meet please get in touch

I hired him immediately. Only a fool wouldn't employ a guy with an Astra

If I read one more application form that states the applicant is "equally happy working on their own or as part of a team" I will scream. I'm going to put that theory to the test one of these days and single man them for thirteen hours a day, seven days a week which reminds me that you also need to be prepared for single manning.

Ah a double edged sword of contention if ever there was one with strong views on both sides. Commercially it is cheaper to single man and, in most shops, doesn't affect customer service. Some staff, given the alternative of working with a moron, actually volunteer for it. Morally, however, is it right to expect somebody to work on their own for up to 13 hours? There are practicalities to consider, of course, such as going for a whizz. Up until there were betting events going off every 60 seconds this was easier to plan. It was considered fairly safe to visit the can as the first fence was being jumped in a 3m 2f race at

Sedgefield. These days, however, a bladder emptying trip can seriously disrupt the smooth running of the shop. You can bet your bottom dollar that, if your wee co-incides with the 4.01 at Youcouldn'tmakeitup Downs then, almost certainly, Big Mouth Billy would have got the tricast up and you, and your inability to literally hold your own piss, would have cost him several hundred pounds.

As with all staffing considerations the safety of the staff should be paramount.

There is a shop in Manchester, in a particularly dodgy area that has all the security measures known to man. A pod entry system that allows staff to buzz people in, kick-ass bandit screen, thick security doors, panic buttons and a state of the art CCTV system. How, then, did the shop come to be robbed at gunpoint? Well, what can't be legislated for is the stupidity of people and, in particular, the shop manager who decided to open the back door, which was behind the counter, and have a sneaky ciggy. On opening said door he was greeted with the startling sight of two men, faces covered, pointing a gun in his direction. They duly pushed him back behind the counter and emptied the safe.

The back door, secured by bolts and locks, was the fire exit only so whose fault was it that the shop was robbed? Did the shop manager deserve sympathy or a right royal kick up the arse?

Robberies, thankfully, are few and far between and most of them are over in under a minute or two though the effects on the staff involved can be much longer lasting.

On a busy Saturday afternoon in a Liverpool shop several years ago the 3 staff members were hard at work when they heard a bang coming from the kitchen area. The manager went to investigate and was rather surprised to see a leg dangling from the ceiling. Without thinking he grabbed hold of it and thus ensued a tussle which resulted in the shoe coming off in the manager's hand. The leg promptly disappeared through the ceiling. In a curious reworking of Cinderella the offender was later matched to his lost shoe and convicted. Transpired he and his pals had actually intended to rob the newsagents next door but took a wrong turn by the air vent.

There was also the time when a disgruntled lunatic of a customer, when he didn't get his own way on a bet, returned to the shop later on with a bag full of live cockroaches and released them into the shop. It was months before the shop was finally clear of the little buggers.

Spare a thought, too, for the shop workers who were pelted with baby new potatoes stolen from the greengrocer next door when they, correctly, applied a Rule 4 to his bet. Good job it wasn't Halloween as pumpkins could really have caused some damage.

In the event of a robbery staff are encouraged to give the offender whatever money is available to get them out of the shop as quickly as possible. This instruction, however, is often ignored and usually by the most unlikely of staff.

In a betting shop on the outskirts of Manchester City Centre there worked a lady called Sheila. Sheila was a cashier in her late 50's with frizzy, greying hair, thick glasses and a nervous habit of doing a little laugh at the end of every sentence. She was non-descript in every way and walked in her sensible shoes with her head down. I think, though, that Sheila also had some secret agent training in her background such was her magnificent response when faced with a would be perp. On a summer's day in the late 90's Sheila was looking for a cash shortage and, in those days, it was more time consuming to check everything and the constant customer interruptions weren't helping. Throw in the fact that the air-con wasn't working and poor Sheila was suffering hot flushes and it was a recipe for disaster. At around this time a guy in a balaclava came in the shop and brandished a shotgun at Sheila demanding she gave him the money. The manager ducked under his desk and shouted at Sheila to get down. But did she? Not on your nelly. Sheila, literally, stared down the barrel of a gun and told the guy to "fuck off". Amazingly he did and Sheila entered the betting shop legend's hall of fame.

There are happenings and strange goings on in betting shops that even Tim Burton wouldn't touch. Stuff so scary and unnatural that Quentin Tarantino would politely pass on. I have thought for several years, now, that a sitcom based in a betting shop would be a huge hit but, then, wonder if it is just shop staff that would see the funny side. The non-initiated viewing public and TV critics would doubtless deem it farfetched but, if Channel 5 feel like giving it a whirl, I'm happy to be the expert consultant.

The "One with the Mouse" would be a particular favourite episode. Several years ago, in a none too salubrious part of Liverpool, there was a shop frequented by an uneasy mix of older regulars with limited tolerance levels and younger, drug addled maniacs with limited respect for anyone. One of these smack heads, for some reason known only to himself and maybe not even that, decided, on a busy Saturday afternoon, to buy a white mouse from the local pet shop and bring it to the shop. Unbeknownst to cantankerous old Jack, who was sat deep in thought studying the form in the Daily Mirror, said smack head very gently placed the mouse on Jack's shoulder and retreated. The mouse froze. Jack didn't move. The rest of the shop was in stitches as the minutes ticked by. The smack head returned to the mouse, picked it up and placed it in Jack's coat pocket. Cue further hilarity as Old Jack continued to write his bets out completely oblivious that he had a rodents head poking out of his pocket. As it turned out Jack only discovered his new pet when he was in the ale house and went to pay for his pint and, instead of pulling out a fiver, pulled out a confused, white mouse which he duly returned to the rather bemused pet shop keeper.

The same smack head, Paul, and his equally drug dependent mate, Eddie, would use the betting shop toilets to score a fix and, though this wasn't encouraged, it wasn't really tackled either. One day, however, a few minutes after Paul and Eddy went to the toilet, there was a thud so loud that the shop manager sent the cashier to investigate (well you don't keep a dog and bark yourself do you?).

The cashier duly returned, completely unfazed, and continued taking bets. "What was it?" the manager asked "Smack head dead on the floor" he shrugged

As the shop manager rang for an ambulance Paul scurried out of the toilet and left the shop.

As it transpired Eddy wasn't dead. Very unwell but definitely not dead. He was taken away by ambulance with bleeding from his head where he had bounced it off the tiled floor when he collapsed. Four days later, before the shop opened, the manager heard the letterbox being lifted and heard Paul shout "Eddy. Eddy? Are you still in there?"

I hope you have enjoyed this little journey through the quirky, wondrous world of betting shops and look forward to seeing you for Part Two where we will explore in further detail the psyche of the betting shop staff. I've checked on Amazon and no other person in the world has written on this unique subject. There will be sarcasm, there will be intrigue, there will be comradeship and resilience in bucket loads.

Until then may the odds be ever in your favour.

Printed in Great Britain
by Amazon